The Runaway Road

by Stan Mack

PARENTS
MAGAZINE
PRESS

NEW YORK

Library of Congress Cataloging in Publication Data
Mack, Stanley.
The runaway road.
SUMMARY: On their way to the mountains for their
annual vacation, the Puddle family take the usual road
but the road seems to have other ideas about where it
wants to go.
[1. Roads—Fiction]   I. Title
PZ7.M1899Ru   [E]   79–5265
ISBN 0–8193–1017–4   ISBN 0–8193–1018–2 lib. bdg.

The Runaway Road

It was time for the
Puddle Family's summer vacation.
Every year they packed up their car
and drove north to the mountains,
where they spent two weeks.

"Is everybody ready?" asked Mr. Puddle.
"Yes," said Mrs. Puddle.
"Yes," said Bobby Puddle.
"Yes," said Jenny Puddle.
"Then off we go!"

They drove through town
and turned onto Route 100.

"Good old Route 100," said **Mr. Puddle**.
"Every year it takes us straight
to the mountains."

Suddenly, the road turned sharply
to the left.
"Strange," said Mrs. Puddle.
"This road doesn't seem as straight
as it did last year."

Route 100 ran over a hill
and through Jane Jones's backyard.
So did the Puddle Family.

"Either somebody moved these houses, or this road is taking a shortcut," said Jenny.

Route 100 rushed back through town.
"We're heading for the South Bridge!"
yelled Bobby.

Route 100 rushed across the bridge
and through the tollbooth.
"You didn't pay your toll!"
shouted the toll collector.

But the road didn't stop,
and the Puddle Family COULDN'T stop.
Police Officer Daley turned on his siren
and began chasing the runaway road.

Route 100 raced along the highway,
jumped a low fence,
and cut across Farmer Brown's fields.

The road bumped Bernard the pig
right up onto the hood of the Puddles' car.
Farmer Brown jumped on his tractor
and took off after them.

Jenny and Bobby saw a diner up ahead.
"I'm hungry," they both said.
And for a minute, Route 100 slowed down.

"Four hot dogs with mustard and
relish to go, please," called Mr. Puddle.
"Coming up," shouted Pierre the cook.
They grabbed the hot dogs just as
the road sped off again.

"Hey, you didn't pay for those
hot dogs!" shouted Pierre.
But the Puddles couldn't stop.

Everyone at the diner
piled into the cook's truck
and joined the chase.

Soon lots of people were following
the Puddles. But no one knew
where they were headed.

Suddenly, they saw the ocean.
"Route 100 is heading for the beach,"
said Officer Daley into his radio.

People stood with their mouths open and watched
as Route 100 ran down Main Street,
over the boardwalk, across the sand . . .
and STOPPED.

"The ocean!" said Jenny.
"I'm going wading."
"And I'm going to build
a giant sand castle," said Bobby.
"Okay," said Mrs. Puddle,
"but be careful."
The children jumped out of the car.

Jane Jones took her dress back.
Farmer Brown rescued Bernard the pig.
Pierre the cook got his money.
And Officer Daley wondered how
to give a traffic ticket to a road.

Then the mayor arrived.
"This road doesn't belong here,"
he said.
"It usually goes to the mountains,"
said Mr. Puddle.

"Here comes Miles McAdam,"
said the mayor.
"He'll know what to do.
He helped build the road."

"Why did the road come to the beach?"
asked the mayor.
"I don't know," said Miles.
"It IS a clever road, isn't it?"
"If the road's so clever,
then ask IT," said the mayor.

So Miles asked the road.
"Yes, that's it," he said finally.
"Route 100 says it is tired of going
to the mountains all the time.

It's come to the seashore
for a vacation. It's having fun!"

Mrs. Puddle had an idea. She said,
"How about if the road stays for
two weeks and then goes back to
the mountains?"

"Good idea!" said the mayor.
"Good idea!" said Miles.
And the road agreed.

And now if you look at a road map,
you'll see a note which says:

ROUTE 100 GOES

TO THE MOUNTAINS

EVERY DAY OF

THE YEAR EXCEPT

THE FIRST TWO

WEEKS IN AUGUST.

Then it goes to the seashore
for its vacation.
And the Puddle Family
always goes with it.

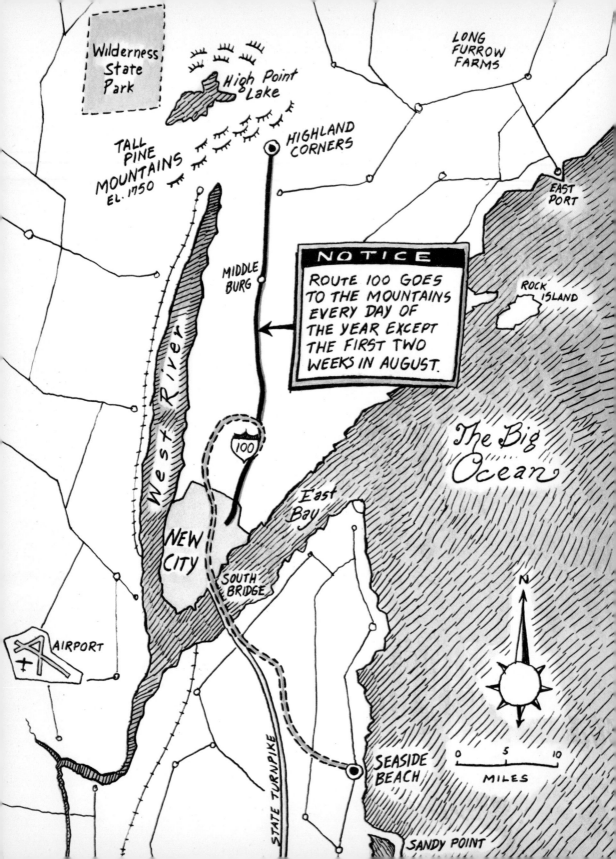